DAVID

Plays Hide-and-Seek in Celebrations

Juega al Escondite en Celebraciones

by Dolores Mayorga

Translated from the Spanish
by Lori Ann Schatschneider

Lerner Publications Company • Minneapolis

This edition published 1992
by Lerner Publications Company
241 First Avenue North
Minneapolis, Minnesota 55401 USA

Originally published as *David juega al escondite y se divierte*
by Editorial Planeta, S.A., Barcelona, Spain
© Dolores Mayorga, 1989

Translation copyright © 1992 by Lerner Publications Company
Translated from the Spanish by Lori Ann Schatschneider

Library of Congress Cataloging-in-Publication Data

Mayorga, Dolores.
    [David juega al escondite y se divierte. English & Spanish]
    David plays hide-and-seek in celebrations = David juega
al escondite en celebraciones / by Dolores Mayorga ;
translated from the Spanish by Lori Ann Schatschneider.
        p.   cm.
    Translation of: David juega al escondite y se divierte.
    Summary: The reader may search for David, his friend,
and other things in depictions of celebrations during each
season of the year.
    ISBN 0-8225-2001-X
    [1. Seasons—Fiction. 2. Picture puzzles. 3. Spanish
language materials—Bilingual.] I. Title. II. Title: David
juega al escondite en celebraciones.
PZ73.M34   1992
[Fic]—dc20   91-48044
                                                       CIP
                                                        AC

Manufactured in the United States of America

1 2 3 4 5 6 7 8 9 10 01 00 99 98 97 96 95 94 93 92

David plays hide-and-seek through the celebrations of autumn, winter, spring, and summer. Mr. Lena the mail carrier and Norma, with her dog, also try to pass by unnoticed.

David juega al escondite a través de las celebraciones de otoño, invierno, primavera, y verano. Sr. Lena el cartero y Norma, con su perro, procuran pasar inadvertidos también.

David has fun
celebrating his
friend's birthday!

*¡David se divierte celebrando
el cumpleaños de
su amigo!*

◆◆◆◆◆◆◆◆◆◆◆◆◆◆◆◆◆◆◆◆◆◆◆◆

David, Mr. Lena, and Norma are
hiding. Can you find them and
these other things too?

*David, Sr. Lena, y Norma se
esconden. ¿Puedes encontrar a ellos
y estas otras cosas también?*

◆◆◆◆◆◆◆◆◆◆◆◆◆◆◆◆◆◆◆◆◆◆◆◆

blind man's bluff
gallina ciega

noisemakers
trompas

five napkins
cinco servilletas

piñata
piñata

cookies
galletas

four apples
cuatro manzanas

cat
gato

sack race
carrera de sacos

oven
horno

Witches and ghosts
go out on Halloween.

*Salen las brujas y los
fantasmas en la víspera
de Todos los Santos.*

◆◆◆◆◆◆◆◆◆◆◆◆◆◆◆◆◆◆◆◆◆◆◆◆◆◆◆

David, Mr. Lena, and Norma
are hiding. Can you find them
and these other things too?

*David, Sr. Lena, y Norma se
esconden. ¿Puedes encontrar a ellos
y estas otras cosas también?*

◆◆◆◆◆◆◆◆◆◆◆◆◆◆◆◆◆◆◆◆◆◆◆◆◆◆◆

graveyard
cementerio

black cats
gatos negros

skeleton
esqueleto

moon
luna

two lizards
dos lagartos

pumpkin
calabaza

spider
araña

horseman
jinete

green hair
pelo verde

The Christmas season
is a time for giving.

*Las Navidades son
una época para dár.*

✦✦✦✦✦✦✦✦✦✦✦✦✦✦✦✦✦✦✦✦✦✦✦✦✦✦

David, Mr. Lena, and Norma
are hiding. Can you find them
and these other things too?

*David, Sr. Lena, y Norma se
esconden. ¿Puedes encontrar a ellos
y estas otras cosas también?*

✦✦✦✦✦✦✦✦✦✦✦✦✦✦✦✦✦✦✦✦✦✦✦✦✦✦

sled
trineo

wreaths
guirnaldas

four stockings
cuatro calcetas

carolers
cantantes de villancicos

elves
duendes

piano
piano

mufflers
bufandas

snowballs
pelotas de nieve

Santa Claus
San Nicolás

When the clock strikes midnight, everyone celebrates the new year.

Cuando el reloj suena a la medianoche, todos celebran el año nuevo.

◆◆◆◆◆◆◆◆◆◆◆◆◆◆◆◆◆◆◆◆◆◆◆◆

David, Mr. Lena, and Norma are hiding. Can you find them and these other things too?

David, Sr. Lena, y Norma se esconden. ¿Puedes encontrar a ellos y estas otras cosas también?

◆◆◆◆◆◆◆◆◆◆◆◆◆◆◆◆◆◆◆◆◆◆◆◆

sailors
marineros

champagne
champaña

grapes
uvas

walking cane
bastón

anchor
ancla

mirror
espejo

waves
ondas

portholes
portas

swiss cheese
queso sueco

Everyone wears a costume in the Mardi Gras parade.

Todos se disfrazan para el desfile de Carnaval.

◆◆◆◆◆◆◆◆◆◆◆◆◆◆◆◆◆◆◆◆◆◆◆◆◆◆

David, Mr. Lena, and Norma are hiding. Can you find them and these other things too?

David, Sr. Lena, y Norma se esconden. ¿Puedes encontrar a ellos y estas cosas también?

◆◆◆◆◆◆◆◆◆◆◆◆◆◆◆◆◆◆◆◆◆◆◆◆◆◆

princess
princesa

mummy
momia

Pink Panther
Pantera Rosa

three mermaids
tres sirenas

knight
caballero

monkey
mono

devil
diablo

flute
flauta

lion
león

It is Easter! David
and his friends look
for painted eggs.

*¡Llega la Pascua!
David y sus amigos
buscan huevos pintados.*

•••••••••••••••••••••••••••••••••

David, Mr. Lena, and Norma
are hiding. Can you find them
and these other things too?

*David, Sr. Lena, y Norma se
esconden. ¿Puedes encontrar a ellos
y estas otras cosas también?*

•••••••••••••••••••••••••••••••••

palm branches
palmones

four rabbits
cuatro conejos

sundial
reloj de sol

pastry shop
pastelería

chocolate eggs
huevos de chocolate

pink bow
lazo rosado

Easter baskets
cestas de Pascua

striped shirt
camisa rayada

two cows
dos vacas

Congratulations to
the bride and groom
on their wedding day.

*Felicidades a los novios
en el día de su boda.*

◆◆◆◆◆◆◆◆◆◆◆◆◆◆◆◆◆◆◆◆◆◆◆◆◆◆◆◆◆

David, Mr. Lena, and Norma
are hiding. Can you find them
and these other things too?

*David, Sr. Lena, y Norma se
esconden. ¿Puedes encontrar a ellos
y estas otras cosas también?*

◆◆◆◆◆◆◆◆◆◆◆◆◆◆◆◆◆◆◆◆◆◆◆◆◆◆◆◆◆

pearl necklace
collar de perlas

four violinists
cuatro violinistas

chef
cocinero

handkerchief
pañuelo

cigar
cigarro

wedding cake
pastel de boda

bouquet of flowers
ramillete de flores

suspenders
tirantes

top hat
sombrero de copa

Fireworks light up the
sky with bright colors.

*Fuegos artificiales
iluminan el cielo con
colores brillantes.*

••••••••••••••••••••••••••

David, Mr. Lena, and Norma
are hiding. Can you find them
and these other things too?

*David, Sr. Lena, y Norma se
esconden. ¿Puedes encontrar a ellos
y estas otras cosas también?*

••••••••••••••••••••••••••

pajamas
pijama

sparks
chispas

bonfire
fogata

rockets
cohetes

match
fósforo

doorbell
timbre de puerta

burned finger
dedo quemado

old woman
anciana

four pizzas
cuatro pizzas

David loves to go
to the fair.

*A David le encanta
ir a la feria.*

••••••••••••••••••••••••••

David, Mr. Lena, and Norma
are hiding. Can you find them
and these other things too?

*David, Sr. Lena, y Norma se
esconden. ¿Puedes encontrar a ellos
y estas otras cosas también?*

••••••••••••••••••••••••••

trampoline
cama elástica

merry-go-round
tiovivo

two clowns
dos payasos

drums
tambores

puppets
títeres

prizes
premios

microphone
micrófono

blindfold
vendado

dancers
bailadores

Our team wins! We
are the champions!

¡Gana nuestro equipo!
¡Somos los campeones!

••••••••••••••••••••••••••••

David, Mr. Lena, and Norma
are hiding. Can you find them
and these other things too?

David, Sr. Lena, y Norma se
esconden. ¿Puedes encontrar a ellos
y estas otras cosas también?

••••••••••••••••••••••••••••

hero
héroe

two hugs
dos embrazos

eyeglasses
gafas

silver cup
copa de plata

two bus drivers
dos conductores

gold medal
medalla de oro

canary
canario

sleeping boy
chico durmiente

blue cap
gorra azul

About the Author and Illustrator

Dolores Mayorga lives in Barcelona, Spain, with her husband and three children, where she writes and illustrates children's books. Her favorite celebration is Easter. She has fun decorating Easter eggs with her children, and she really likes to eat chocolate candy eggs.

Sobre la Autora y Artisa

Dolores Mayorga vive en Barcelona, España, con su esposo y sus tres hijos, donde escribe y ilustra libros para niños. Su celebración favorito es la Pascua. Se divierte decorando huevos de Pascua con sus hijos, y a ella le gusta comer los dulces huevos de chocolate.